MW01153041

DISCARD

THE DANGERS OF DRUGS, ALCOHOL, AND SMOKING

THE DANGERS OF
OPIOIDS

DAVID KLIMCHUK

PowerKiDS
press
New York

Published in 2020 by The Rosen Publishing Group, Inc.
29 East 21st Street, New York, NY 10010

Copyright © 2020 by The Rosen Publishing Group, Inc.

All rights reserved. No part of this book may be reproduced in any form without permission in writing from the publisher, except by a reviewer.

First Edition

Editor: Jenna Tolli
Book Design: Reann Nye

Photo Credits: Cover Monkey Business Images/Shutterstock.com; series art patpitchaya/Shutterstock.com; p. 5 Burlingham/Shutterstock.com; p. 7 RimDream/Shutterstock.com; p. 8 Daisy-Daisy/iStock/Getty Images Plus/Getty Images; p. 9 TEK IMAGE/SCIENCE PHOTO LIBRARY/Science Photo Library/Getty Images; p. 11 New2me86/Shutterstock.com; p. 13 fizkes/Shutterstock.com; p. 14 Tom Wang/Shutterstock.com; p. 15 Brent Stirton/ Getty Images News/Getty Images; p. 17 PureRadiancePhoto/Shutterstock.com; p. 19 Caiaimage/Tom Merton/Caiaimage/Getty Images; p. 21 Ivonne Wierink/Shutterstock.com; p. 22 Rawpixel.com/Shutterstock.com.

Cataloging-in-Publication Data

Names: Klimchuk, David.
Title: The dangers of opioids / David Klimchuk.
Description: New York : PowerKids Press, 2020. | Series: The dangers of drugs, alcohol, and smoking | Includes glossary and index.
Identifiers: ISBN 9781725309821 (pbk.) | ISBN 9781725309845 (library bound) | ISBN 9781725309838 (6 pack)
Subjects: LCSH: Opioid abuse–Juvenile literature. | Opioids–Juvenile literature. | Drug abuse–Juvenile literature.
Classification: LCC RC568.O45 K585 2020 | DDC 616.86–dc23

Manufactured in the United States of America

Some of the images in this book illustrate individuals who are models. The depictions do not imply actual situations or events.

CPSIA Compliance Information: Batch #CWPK20. For Further Information contact Rosen Publishing, New York, New York at 1-800-237-9932.

CONTENTS

WHAT ARE OPIOIDS?

Opioids are **addictive** drugs and can be very dangerous, or harmful. Pills like hydrocodone or oxycodone are opioids that help with pain **relief**. There are also opioid "street drugs", like heroin, which are illegal. All opioids come from the opium poppy plant which usually grows in places with warm, dry climates, such as Pakistan and Mexico.

In the United States, opioid misuse has become a serious public health **crisis** and the number of opioid-related deaths has been rising. How does this drug cause addiction, and what can you do if someone in your life is addicted to opioids?

DANGER ZONE

Opioids like morphine and codeine were used for pain relief as early as 1803. Both drugs are made from the opium poppy plant.

JONATHAN DOE

℞

TAKE AS NEEDED

RX 2823357-15066

QTY **30**

12 REFILLS BEFORE 4/11/15

Pharmacy

It is legal to use pain pills that a doctor **prescribes** to you as directed. But taking pills that were prescribed to someone else is illegal.

DIFFERENT KINDS OF OPIOIDS

There are many different types of opioids that could lead to addiction or accidental death. Heroin is a popular street drug, which has nicknames like "horse" or "smack." It can be smoked, breathed in through the nose, or taken by a needle. Heroin is usually sold in powder form. People might turn to heroin after they run out of pain medicine because it has similar, but stronger, effects.

Most recently, there has been an increase in the use of **synthetic** opioids, such as the drug fentanyl. They are responsible for the most drug-related deaths. Fentanyl creates a much bigger "**high**" than other opioids and can be added to other drugs.

DANGER ZONE

Opioids are a depressant drug, also known as "downers." This means they make body activities slow down. This includes slurred or unclear speech, slower breathing, and brain problems.

Many people who take opioids for pain never think they could get addicted, but this is how many addictions begin.

HOW THE BRAIN WORKS

Opioid addiction has a lot to do with how the human brain works. Opioids attach to different areas of the brain and body, which are known as "opioid **receptors**." When this happens, **chemicals** that help people feel good are released, or let out. After people have these feelings, their brains and bodies want to have them again. This is how addiction starts.

DANGER ZONE

Making smart choices about not using drugs is important for all ages. For kids, dangerous drugs like opioids can be especially unsafe and can even change how their brain forms.

8

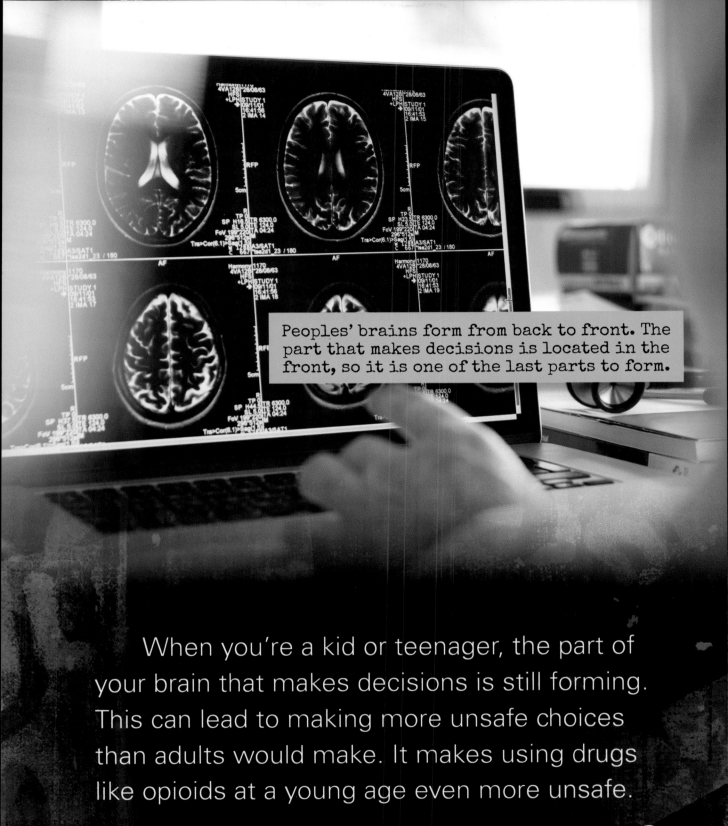

Peoples' brains form from back to front. The part that makes decisions is located in the front, so it is one of the last parts to form.

When you're a kid or teenager, the part of your brain that makes decisions is still forming. This can lead to making more unsafe choices than adults would make. It makes using drugs like opioids at a young age even more unsafe.

OVERDOSES

Like many drugs, if a person uses too much of an opioid, they could have an **overdose**. Sometimes overdoses can be deadly. Although people can overdose on any type of opioid, the one that most often leads to death is fentanyl. This drug is most dangerous when it is mixed into someone's heroin or other drug without them knowing.

Signs that someone may be overdosing include: throwing up, their fingernails turning black or blue, and not being able to talk. They might also stop breathing and pass out. If someone doesn't help them in the first five minutes, the lack of oxygen could cause serious brain problems or death.

DANGER ZONE

Luckily, a life-saving medication called naloxone was created to help treat an opioid overdose. Many communities have trainings to teach people how to use naloxone.

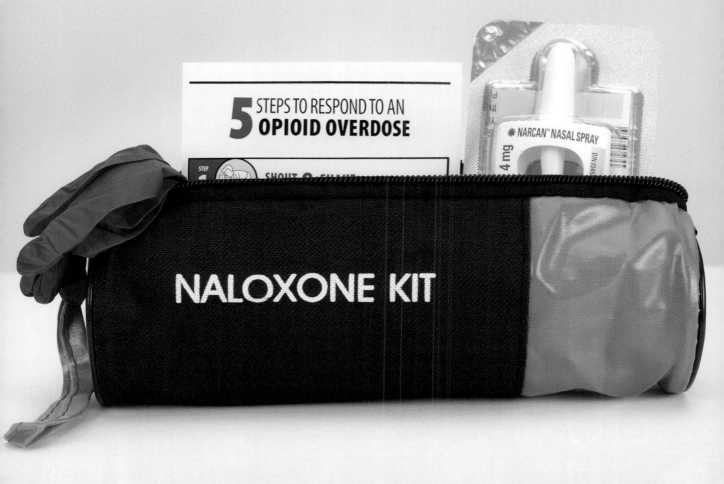

The drug naloxone helps police, **emergency** responders, doctors, and family members save lives when someone overdoses on opioids.

5 STEPS TO RESPOND TO AN **OPIOID OVERDOSE**

NALOXONE KIT

SIGNS OF ADDICTION

It's usually very hard to notice when someone is starting an opioid addiction. People who have problems using drugs like opioids become skilled at hiding their struggles from loved ones. If someone is starting to act differently, you might notice a few signs.

Someone with an addiction might not enjoy some of the same things they used to. They may have big mood changes, like getting angry quickly. You might also see them do things they normally wouldn't do, like lying or keeping secrets. People with an opioid addiction might steal pills from family members, or take money to buy more pills.

People with opioid addictions may avoid people they love and might stop going to school or work. If someone you know is having these problems, tell an adult you trust.

13

MYTHS ABOUT ADDICTION

Opioid problems often start after people use legal medicines that doctors prescribed for pain. People can become addicted to opioids even if they only use the drugs as the doctor suggested they should.

DANGER ZONE

Another myth about opioids is that only certain types of people are at risk for addiction. Certain factors can put people at higher risk, but anyone can be affected.

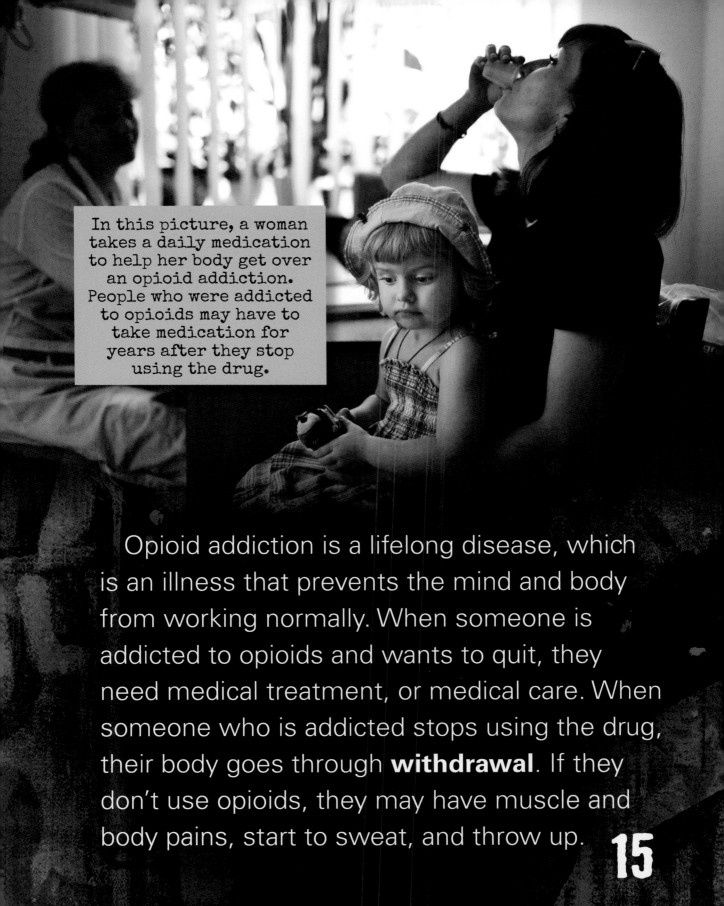

In this picture, a woman takes a daily medication to help her body get over an opioid addiction. People who were addicted to opioids may have to take medication for years after they stop using the drug.

Opioid addiction is a lifelong disease, which is an illness that prevents the mind and body from working normally. When someone is addicted to opioids and wants to quit, they need medical treatment, or medical care. When someone who is addicted stops using the drug, their body goes through **withdrawal**. If they don't use opioids, they may have muscle and body pains, start to sweat, and throw up.

15

TREATING WITH MEDICATION

What happens after someone is **diagnosed** with opioid addiction? Their treatment usually includes special medications that will help them quit and manage side effects. They might also go to individual and group counseling for advice and support.

Medicines like methadone can be used to help people stop their opioid addiction. A doctor prescribes them. They block the "high" opioids can cause and reduce how much those with an addiction want the drug. They also help people as they go through withdrawal so they don't have such painful side effects. People might need to be on these medications for years or even their entire lives.

16

DANGER ZONE

When people are getting the opioids out of their bodies at the beginning of treatment, it is called detoxification, or "detox." Trying to detox without medical help is very dangerous.

There are still risks when taking medications like methadone. Doctors work closely with patients to find the best way to treat their opioid addiction.

COUNSELING

Along with medication, counseling is important for helping opioid addictions. Some people need to go away to a treatment center, where they stay and get medical care for weeks or months.

Other people are able to live at home while they quit opioids, but they have to go to one-on-one treatment and group counseling. Their counselor will ask them to take drug tests regularly to make sure they haven't started using opioids again. A very important part of treatment involves psychoeducation. This is when people learn more about how their addiction works, how to cope, and different skills to help them quit.

Group counseling gives people the chance to share their stories with others who have had similar experiences.

19

struggling with it.

If you think someone you know could be having a problem with using opioids, tell an adult you trust. Parents, teachers, and counselors can help you find out what to do next.

It can be scary when someone you know becomes addicted to opioids. Sometimes people feel ashamed and might not reach out for help.

>

21

AVOIDING ADDICTION

It's easier for young people to become addicted to opioids because their brains are still developing. Unfortunately, many opioid addictions start when someone has been using a pain medicine that was prescribed after getting seriously hurt or having an operation. This is why it's very important to work with your doctor to find the best ways to manage pain.

Kids who stay in school and get involved in healthy activities are usually at lower risk of addiction. Find ways to stay involved and be active! Making smart choices when you're young will help you stay safe and avoid these dangerous drugs.

GLOSSARY

addictive: Something that causes someone to not want to stop.

chemicals: Matter that can be mixed with other matter to cause changes.

crisis: An unstable or difficult situation.

diagnosed: Identified by certain signs.

emergency: An unexpected and unsafe situation that needs quick action.

high: Intoxicated or affected by alcohol or drug use.

overdose: Too much of a substance like a medicine or illegal drug that is dangerous.

prescribe: To officially tell someone to use a medicine or treatment.

receptor: A nerve ending that senses changes in light, temperature, or pressure, and makes the body react in a certain way.

relief: Removing or reducing of something that is painful or unpleasant.

synthetic: Something that is not made in nature.

withdrawal: Physical and mental problems that happen after a person stops using an addictive drug.

23

INDEX

WEBSITES

Due to the changing nature of Internet links, PowerKids Press has developed an online list of websites related to the subject of this book. This site is updated regularly. Please use this link to access the list: www.powerkidslinks.com/das/opioids